John P. Hobler, London Glee Club

The Words of the Favourite Pieces

as performed at the Glee club, held at the Crown and Anchor tavern,

Strand

John P. Hobler, London Glee Club

The Words of the Favourite Pieces
as performed at the Glee club, held at the Crown and Anchor tavern, Strand

ISBN/EAN: 9783337270674

Printed in Europe, USA, Canada, Australia, Japan

Cover: Foto ©Andreas Hilbeck / pixelio.de

More available books at **www.hansebooks.com**

THE
WORDS

OF THE

FAVOURITE PIECES,

AS PERFORMED AT THE

GLEE CLUB,

HELD AT THE

CROWN AND ANCHOR TAVERN,

𝔖𝔱𝔯𝔞𝔫𝔡.

COMPILED from their LIBRARY,

BY

J. PAUL HOBLER.

―――――

——— We fpend the focial Night,
Still mixing Profit with Delight.   HOR. SAT.

―――――

LONDON.
PRINTED for the EDITOR.

Sold by H. D. SYMONDS, Pater Nofter Row;
and to be had at the Place of Meeting.

1794.

TO THE

PRESIDENT

AND

GENTLEMEN,

SUBSCRIBERS TO THE

GLEE CLUB,

THIS BOOK is humbly dedicated, with a View to increaſe the Hilarity of their Meetings, by

Their moſt obedient,

And devoted Servant,

J. PAUL HOBLER.

October, 1794.

Favourite Pieces, &c.

INTRODUCTORY GLEE,

3 Voices and Chorus,

Written and compofed exprefsly for the Club,

By Samuel Webbe.

GLORIOUS Apollo from on high beheld us,
    Wand'ring to find a temple for his praife,
Sent Polyhymnia hither to fhield us,
    While we ourfelves fuch a ftructure might raife.
        Thus then combining,
        Hands and hearts joining,
    Sing we in harmony Apollo's praife.

Here ev'ry gen'rous fentiment awaking,
    Mufic infpiring unity and joy ;
Each focial pleafure giving and partaking,
    Glee and good-humour our hours employ.
        Thus then combining,
        Hands and hearts joining,
    Long may continue our unity and joy.

GLEE, 3 Voc. Dr. Rogers.

COME, come all noble fouls, who fkill'd in mufic's art,
    Do join in this fociety to bear a part;
For in this pleafant grove we'll fit, we'll drink, and fing,
And imitate thofe cheerful birds now in the fpring;
The Mufes nine fhall know, and all moft plainly fee,
Our off'ring at their fhrine is love and harmony.

GLEE, 5 Voc. Battishill,

AMIDST the myrtles as I walk,
    Love and myfelf thus enter talk;
Tell me, faid I, in deep diftrefs,
Where I may find my fhepherdefs?

A 5 Voc. Webbe.

A Gen'rous friendfhip no cold medium knows,
    Burns with one love, with one refentment glows;
One fhould our intereft and our paffion be,
My friend fhould hate the man that injures me.

A 4 Voc. Stafford Smith.

AS on a fummer's day,
    In a green-wood fhade as I lay;
    The maid that I lov'd,
    As her fancy mov'd,
Came walking forth that way:

And as she passed by
With a scornful glance of her eye,
  What a shame, quoth she,
  For a Swain must it be,
Like a lazy loon for to lie.
And dost thou nothing heed
What Pan our god has decreed?
  What a prize to-day
  Shall be giv'n away
To the sweetest shepherd's reed:
  There's scarce a single swain,
  Of all this fruitful plain,
    But with hopes and fears,
    Now busily prepares
The bonny boon to gain.
Shall another maiden shine
In brighter array than thine,
  Up, up, dull swain, and make the garland mine.

A 3 Voc. WEBBE.

AS o'er the varied meads I stray,
  Or trace thro' winding woods my way;
While op'ning flow'rs their sweets exhale,
And odours breathe in ev'ry gale:
Where sage Contentment builds her seat,
And Peace attends the calm retreat;
My soul responsive hails the scene,
Attun'd to joy and peace within.
But, musing on the lib'ral hand
That scatters blessings o'er the land;

That

That gives for man with pow'r divine,
The earth to teem, the fun to fhine;
My grateful heart with rapture burns,
And pleafure to devotion turns.

GLEE, 4 Voc. DANBY.

AWAKE, Æolian Lyre, awake!
  And give to rapture all thy trembling ftrings;
 From Helicon's harmonious fprings,
A thoufand rills their mazy progrefs take.
The laughing flow'rs that round them blow;
Drink life and fragrance as they flow.
Now the rich ftream of mufic winds along,
Deep, majeftic, fmooth and ftrong,
Through verdant vales and Ceres' golden reign;
Now rolling down the fteep amain,
Headlong impetuous fee it pour;
The rocks and nodding groves re-bellow to the roar.

A 3 Voc. BAILDON.

ADIEU to the village delights
  Which lately my fancy enjoy'd,
No longer the country invites,
 To me all its pleafures are void:
Adieu, thou fweet health breathing hill,
 Thou can'ft not my comfort reftore,
For ever adieu my dear vill,
 My Lucy, alas! is no more.

She,

She, fhe was the caufe of my pain,
  My blefling, my honour, my pride;
She ne'er gave me caufe to complain
  Till that fatal day when fhe dy'd.
Her eyes that fo beautiful fhone
  Are clofed for ever in fleep;
And mine, fince my Lucy is gone,
  Have nothing to do but to weep.

Could my tears the bright angel reftore,
  Like a fountain they never fhould ceafe;
But Lucy, alas! is no more,
  And I am a ftranger to peace;
Let me copy with fervour devout,
  The virtues that glow'd in her heart,
Then foon, when life's fand is run out,
  We may meet again never to part.

A 4 Voc.   Dr. Cooke.

AS now the fhades of eve imbrown
  The fcenes where penfive poets rove;
From care remote, from envy's frown,
  The joys of inward calm I prove.
What holy ftrains around me fwell,
  No wildly rude tumultuous found;
They fix the foul in magic fpell,
  Soft let me tread this favour'd ground.
Sweet is the gale that breathes the fpring,
  Sweet thro' the vale yon winding ftream;
Sweet are the notes love's warblers fing,
  But fweeter friendfhip's folemn theme.

A 5 Voc. Wm. Rock, jun.

ALONE thro' unfrequented wilds,
　　With penfive fteps I rove,
I afk the rocks, I afk the ftreams,
　　Where dwells my abfent love ?
The filent eve, the rofy morn,
　　My conftant fearch furvey,
But who can tell if thou, my dear,
　　Wilt e'er remember me ?

A 5 Voc. Stafford Smith.

BLEST pair of firens, pledges of heav'n's joy,
　　Sphere-born harmonious fifters, voice and verfe,
Wed your divine founds, and mix'd pow'r employ,
　　Dead things with in breath'd fenfe able to pierce ;
And to our high rais'd phantafy prefent
That undifturbed fong of pure confent,
As fung before the faphire-colour'd throne,
To Him that fits thereon,
　　With faintly fhout and folemn jubilee ;
Where the bright Seraphin in burning row,
Their loud uplifted angel-trumpets blow,
And the cherubic hoft in thoufand quires,
Touch their immortal harps of golden wires,
With thofe juft fpirits, that wear victorious palms,
Hymns devout, and holy pfalms
　　Singing everlaftingly :

That

That we on earth with undifcording voice,
May rightly anfwer that melodious noife ;
As once we did, till difproportioned fin
Jarr'd againft nature's chime, and with harfh din
Broke the fair mufic that all creatures made
To their great Lord, whofe love their motion fway'd
In perfect diapafon, while they ftood
In firft obedience, and their ftate of good.
O ! may we foon again renew that fong,
And keep in tune with heav'n, till God, ere long,
To his celeftial concert us unite,
To live with Him, and fing in endlefs morn of light.

A 4 Voc. Webbe.

BREATHE foft ye winds, ye waters gently flow ;
    Shield her ye trees, ye flow'rs around her grow ;
Ye fwains I beg you pafs in filence by,
My love in yonder vale afleep doth lie.

A 3 Voc. Battishill.

CONSIGN'D to duft, beneath this ftone
    In manhood's prime is Damon laid,
Joylefs he liv'd but dy'd unknown
    In bleak misfortune's barren fhade :
Lov'd by the mufe but lov'd in vain,
    'Twas beauty drew his ruin on,
He faw young Daphne on the plain,
    He lov'd, believ'd, and was undone !

Beneath

Beneath this ſtone the youth is laid,
   O ! greet his aſhes with a tear ;
May Heav'n with bleſſings crown his ſhade,
   And grant that peace he wanted here !

A 4 Voc. Dr. Arne.

COME, ſhepherds, we'll follow the hearſe,
   We'll ſee our lov'd Corydon laid ;
Though ſorrow may blemiſh the verſe,
   Yet let the ſoft tribute be paid.

They call'd him the pride of the plain,
   In ſooth he was gentle and kind ;
He mark'd in his elegant ſtrain,
   The graces that glow'd in his mind.

No verdure ſhall cover the vale,
   No bloom on the bloſſoms appear ;
The trees of the foreſt ſhall fail,
   And winter diſcolour the year.

No birds in our hedges ſhall ſing,
   Our hedges ſo vocal before ;
Since he that ſhould welcome the ſpring,
   Can hail the gay ſeaſon no more.

A 4 Voc. Lord Mornington.

COME, fhepherds, come away without delay,
   While the gentle time doth ftay ;
Green woods are dumb, and will never tell to any,
Thofe fweet kiffes, and thofe many
Fond embraces which were giv'n ;
Dainty pleafures that could ev'n
In coldeft age raife a fire,
And give virgins foft defire ;
Come, fhepherds, come away without delay,
While the gentle time doth ftay.

A 4 Voc. Lord Mornington.

COME, faireft nymph, refume thy reign,
   Bring all the graces in thy train ;
With balmy breath and flow'ry head,
Rife from thy foft ambrofial bed ;
Where, in Elyfian flumber bound,
Embow'ring myrtles veil thee round ;
Awake, in all thy glories dreft,
Recall the zephyr from the weft,
Reftore the fun, revive the fkies,
At nature's call and mine, arife ;
Great nature's felf upbraids thy ftay,
And miffes her accuftom'd May.
See, all her works demand thy aid,
The labours of Pomona fade ;

C

A plaint

A plaint is heard from ev'ry tree,
Each budding flow'ret waits for thee.
Come then, with pleafure at thy fide,
Diffufe thy vernal fpirit wide;
Create, where-e'er thou turn'ft thine eye,
Peace, plenty, love, and harmony.

A 4 Voc. WEBBE.

COME live with me, and be my love,
    And we will all the pleafures prove;
That grove and valley, hill and field,
Or woods and fteepy mountains yield.

And I will make thee beds of rofes,
And twine a thoufand fragrant pofies;
A cap of flow'rs, and rural kirtle,
Embroider'd all with leaves of myrtle.

A belt of ftraw and ivy buds,
A coral clafp and amber ftuds;
And if thefe pleafures may thee move,
Then live with me, and be my love.

The fhepherd fwains fhall dance and fing,
For thy delight each May morning;
If joys like thefe thy mind may move,
Then live with me, and be my love.

Answer,

ANSWER.

A 4 Voc. WEBBE.

IF love and all the world were young,
  And truth in ev'ry ſhepherd's tongue;
Thy fancy'd pleaſures might me move,
And I might liſten to thy love.

But time drives flocks from field to fold,
Then rivers rage, and hills grow cold;
Then drooping Philomel is dumb,
And age complains of cares to come.

Thy gowns, thy belts, thy beds of roſes,
Thy cap, thy kirtle, and thy poſies;
All theſe in me can nothing move,
To live with thee, and be thy love.

If youth could laſt, and love ſtill breed,
Had joys no date, and age no need;
Then theſe delights my mind might move,
And I might liſten to thy love.

A 4 Voc. DANBY.

COME, ye party jangling ſwains,
  Leave your flocks, and quit the plains;
Friends to country, friends to court,
Nothing here ſhall ſpoil your ſport;
Ever welcome to our feaſt,
Welcome ev'ry friendly gueſt.

Sprightly

Sprightly widows come away,
Laughing dames, and virgins gay;
Little gaudy, flutt'ring miffes,
Smiling hopes of future bliffes;
Ever welcome to our feaft,
Welcome ev'ry friendly gueft.

All that rip'ning Sun can bring,
Beauteous Summer, beauteous Spring,
In one varying fcene we fhow,
The green, the ripe, the bud, the blow;
Ever welcome to our feaft,
Welcome ev'ry friendly gueft.

Comus jefting, mufic charming,
Wine infpiring, beauty warming;
Rage and party malice dies,
Peace returns, and difcord flies;
Ever welcome to our feaft,
Welcome ev'ry friendly gueft.

A 3 Voc.   HILTON.

COME let us all a Maying go,
    And lightly trip it to and fro:
The bells fhall ring,
And the cuckoo fing;
The drums fhall beat, the fife fhall play,
And fo we'll pafs our time away.

A 4 Voc. RAVENSCROFT.

CAN'ST thou love and lie alone, love is fo difgraced;
    Pleafure is beft when it can reft, in a heart embraced.
Rife, rife, day light, do not burn out;
    Bells now ring, and birds do fing,
'Tis only I that mourn out.

Morning ftar doth now appear,
Wind is hufh'd, and fky is clear:
Come away, come, come away,
Can'ft thou love? then burn out day.

A 3 Voc. FRANCIS IRELAND.

COULD gold prolong my fleeting breath,
    Or guard me from the ftroke of death;
Then would I toil for precious ore,
And amafs a boundlefs ftore.
But fince all at length muft die!
Nor gold a fingle hour can buy;
Let the joys of life be mine,
Pour the ftreams of rofy wine;
Let me tafte in Chloe's arms
All the heav'n of beauty's charms;
The fmiles of friendfhip let me prove,
Friendfhip is the foul of love.

DISCORD, dire fifter of the flaught'ring pow'r,
Small at her birth, but rifing ev'ry hour;
While fcarce the fkies her horrid head can bound,
She ftalks on earth, and fkakes the world around.

But lovely Peace, in angel's form,
Defcending, quells the rifing ftorm;
Soft Eafe and fweet Content fhall reign,
And Difcord never rife again.

A 4 Voc. WEBBE.

DO not afk me, charming Phillis,
Why I lead you here alone;
By this bank of pinks and lillies,
And of rofes newly blown:
'Tis not to behold the beauty
Of thofe flow'rs that crown the fpring,
'Tis to!— but I know my duty,
And dare never name the thing.
'Tis, at worft, but her denying,
Why fhould you thus fearful be?
Ev'ry minute gently flying,
Smiles and fays, make ufe of me.
What the fun does to thofe rofes,
While the beams play fweetly in;
I wou'd!— but my fear oppofes,
And I dare not name the thing.

Yet

Yet I die if I conceal it,
　　Aſk my eyes, or aſk your own;
And if neither can reveal it,
　　Think what lovers do alone.
On this bank of pinks and lillies,
　　Might I ſpeak what I wou'd do;
I wou'd! — with my lovely Phillis,
　　I wou'd! — I wou'd! — Ah! wou'd you?

─────────────

A 5 Voc. WEBBE.

DAUGHTER ſweet of voice and air,
　　Gentle Echo, haſte thee here;
From the vale, where all around,
Rocks to rocks return the ſound:
From the ſwelling ſurge that roars
'Gainſt the tempeſt-beaten ſhores;
From the ſilent moſs-grown cell,
Haunt of warb'ling Philomel:
Where unſeen of man you lie,
Queen of woodland harmony.
Daughter ſweet of voice and air,
Gentle Echo, haſte thee here;
If thou would'ſt Narciſſus move,
To requite thy tender love;
From Delia thou may'ſt learn the art,
She captivates the hardeſt heart.

A 5 Voc. WILBYE.

DOWN in a valley as Alexis trips,
 He faw young Daphne fleeping;
Soon did the wanton touch her ruby lips,
 She blufh'd and fell a weeping.
The youth then gently greets her,
But all in vain entreats her:
Since neither fighs nor tears cou'd move her pity,
With plaint he warbled forth his mournful ditty.

A 4 Voc. FARMER.

FAIR Phillis I faw fitting all alone,
 Feeding her flock, near to the mountain fide;
The fhepherds knew not whither fhe was gone,
 But after her lover Amintas hy'd:
Up and down he wander'd while fhe was miffing,
But when he found her, O then they fell a kiffing.

A 3 Voc. DYNE.

FILL the bowl with rofy wine,
 Around our temples rofes twine;
And let us chearfully awhile,
Like the wine and rofes fmile.
To-day is ours, what do we fear?
To-day is ours, we have it here;

Let's

Let's treat it kindly, that it may
Wifh at leaft with us to ftay:
Let's banifh care, let's banifh forrow,
To the gods belongs to-morrow.

***

A 5 Voc. WILBYE.

FLORA gave me faireft flow'rs,
  None fo fair in Flora's treafure;
Thefe I plac'd in Phillis' bow'rs,
  She was pleas'd, and fhe's my pleafure:
Smiling meadows feem to fay,
Come, ye wantons, here to play.

***

SEQUEL.

5 Voc. ATTERBURY.

I'VE often heard her fay that fhe lov'd pofies;
  In the merry month of May I gave her rofes;
Cowflips and gilly-flow'rs, and the fweet lilly,
I got to deck the bow'rs of my dear Philly.

***

A 4 Voc. DR. COOKE.

FAIR Sufan did her wife hode well maintain,
  Algates affaulted fo, by lovers twaine;
Now an' I reade aright that auncient fong,
The paramours were olde, the dame was young:

D   Had

Had thilk fame tale in other guife been told,
Had they been young and fhe been olde,
Pardie! that wou'd ha' been much forer tryale,
Full marvailous, I wot, were fuch denyale.

A 4 Voc.   THOMAS FORD.

FAIR, fweet, cruel, why doft thy fly me?
   O go not from thy deareft,
Tho' thou doft haften I am nigh thee;
   When thou feem'ft far, then I am neareft:
Tarry then and take me with you.

Fie fweeteft, here is no danger,
   O fly not, love purfues thee;
I am no foe nor foreign ftranger,
   Thy fcorn with frefher hope renews me:
Tarry then and take me with you.

A 3 Voc.   DR. NARES.

FEAR no more the heat of the fun,
   Nor the furious winter's rages,
Thou thy worldly tafk haft done,
   Home art gone to take thy wages;
Golden lads and laffes muft
All follow thee, and turn to duft.
No exorcifer harm thee!
And no witchcraft charm thee!

Ghoft

Ghoft unlaid forbear thee!
Nothing ill come near thee!
Quiet confummation have,
Unremoved be thy grave.

A 3 Voc. DANBY,

FAIR Flora decks the flow'ry ground,
     And plants the bloom of May,
Whilft ev'ry hill, and ev'ry dale,
     Appears unufual gay :
The pretty warblers of the grove
     Affume their various notes ;
Th' echoing woods refponfive found,
     The mufic of their throats.
Lead on, my Celia, quit the town,
     And banifh ev'ry care ;
O hafte, my Celia, hafte away,
     To breathe the rural air.

A 3 Voc. DR. WILSON.

FROM the fair Lavinian fhore,
     I your markets come to ftore ;
Mufe not though fo far I dwell,
And my wares come here to fell :
Such is the facred hunger for gold.
     Then come to my pack,
     While I cry, " What d'ye lack,
What d'ye buy, for here it is to be fold."

I have

I have beaüty, honor, grace,
Fortune, favor, time, and place,
And what elfe thou would'ft requeft,
Ev'n the thing thou likeft beft:
Firft let me have but a touch of your gold,
   Then come to me lad,
   Thou fhalt have what thy dad
Never gave, for here it is to be fold.

Madam, come, fee what you lack,
I've complexions in my pack;
White and red you may have in this place,
To hide your old and wrinkled face.
Firft let me have but a touch of your gold,
   Then thou fhalt feem
   Like a wench of fifteen,
Although you be three fcore and ten years old.

A 3 VOC. CALLCOTT, M. B.

FAREWELL to Lochaber, and farewell my Jean,
   Where heartfome with thee I have many days been;
For Lochaber no more,
May be to return to Lochaber no more.
Thefe tears that I fhed, they are all for my dear,
And not for the dangers attending on war;
Tho' borne on rough feas to a far diftant fhore,
May be to return to Lochaber no more.

A 5 Voc. STAFFORD SMITH.

FLORA now calleth forth each flow'r,
 And bids make ready Maia's bow'r,
 Who ftill doth lie in a trance.
Then will we little love awake,
That now fleepeth in Lethe's lake,
 And pray him leaden our dance.

A 4 Voc. WEBBE, JUN.

FROM peace and focial joy Medufa flies,
 And loves to hear the ftorm of thunder rife :
Thus hags and witches hate the fmiles of day,
Sport in loud thunder, and in tempefts play.

A 5 Voc. WEBBE.

GREAT Bacchus, O aid us to fing thy great glory,
 Thou chief of the gods we affemble before thee:
  Wine's firft projector,
  Mankind's protector;
Hail patron of focial delights ! we adore thee !
All nature rejoic'd when thy birth was declar'd,
Behold here thy altar ! and vot'ries prepar'd ;
  Crown with thy bleffing
  All who confeffing,
No pow'r on earth can with thine be compar'd.

A 4 Voc. Dr. Cooke.

GAYLY I liv'd, as eafe and nature taught,
And fpent may little life without a thought;
And am amaz'd that Death, that tyrant grim,
Shou'd think of me, who never thought of him.

A 4 Voc. Dr. Hayes.

GENTLY touch the warbling lyre,
Chloe feems inclined to reft;
Fill her foul with fond defire,
Softeft notes will footh her breaft,
Pleafing dreams affift in love,
Let them all propitious prove.

A 3 Voc. Dr. Dupuis.

GATHERING violets yefterday,
Alas! my heart was ftole away;
Bell! I've been with thee alone,
Know'ft thou where my heart is gone?
My little fhepherdefs reveal,
Did'ft thou the captive wand'rer fteal?
Then in thy breaft my heart retain,
Or elfe reftore it back again.
But, if my wand'ring heart has flown
To fteal its paffage to thy own,
O! let it take of love its fill,
And I fhall gather violets ftill.

A 3

A 4 Voc. J. W. Callcott, M. B.

GO tuneful bird, that glad'ſt the ſkies,
    To Daphne's window ſpeed thy way;
And there on quiv'ring pinions riſe,
    There thy vocal art diſplay.
And if ſhe deign thy notes to hear,
    And if ſhe praiſe thy matin ſong;
Tell her the ſounds that charm her ear,
    To Damon's native plains belong.

―――――――

A 3 Voc. Brewer.

TURN, Amarillis, to thy ſwain,
    Thy Damon calls thee back again;
Here's a pretty arbour by,
Where Apollo cannot ſpy;
Here let's ſit, and whilſt I play,
Sing to my pipe a roundelay.

―――――――

The Answer.
A 4 Voc. Paxton.

GO Damon go, Amarillis bids adieu,
    Go ſeek another love,
But prove to her more true:
No, no, I care not
For your pretty arbour nigh,
Although great Apollo cannot ſpy:
Nor will I ſit to hear you play,
Nor tune my voice to your roundelay.

A Voc. Alterbury.

GENTLE air, thou breath of lovers,
   Vapour from a secret fire;
Which by thee itself discovers,
   Ere yet daring to aspire:
Softest note of whisper'd anguish,
   Harmony's refined part;
Striking while thou seem'st to languish,
   Full upon the list'ner's heart.

A 4 Voc. Callcott, M. B.

GO, idle boy, I quit thy bow'r,
   Thy couch of many a thorn and flow'r,
I wish thee well for pleasures past,
But bless the hour I'm free at last.
Yet still, methinks, the alter'd day
Scatters around a mournful ray;
And chilling ev'ry zephyr blows,
And ev'ry stream untuneful flows;
Haste thee back then, idle boy,
And with thine anguish bring thy joy:
O rend my heart with ev'ry pain,
But let me, let me—love again.

A 3 Voc. MICHAEL ESTE.

HOW merrily we live that shepherds be;
   Roundelays still we sing with merry glee:
On the pleasant downs, where, as our flocks we see,
We feel no cares, we feel not fortune's frowns:
We have no envy which sweet mirth confounds.

A 3 Voc. DR. ARNE.

HUSH to peace each ruder wind,
   Purling rills in silence roll,
While on rosy bed reclin'd
   Sleeps the charmer of my soul.

Chaste Diana, watch my treasure,
   Guard her beauty from alarms ;
Let no satyr's brutal pleasure
   Dare invade her blooming charms.

Somnus, God of balmy rest,
   Sweetly slumb'ring let her prove
Ev'ry joy that Strephon blest,
   Cou'd bestow in waking love.

A 4 Voc. DR. COOKE.

HOW sleep the brave, who sink to rest,
   By all their country's wishes blest !
When spring with dewy fingers cold,
Returns to deck their hallow'd mould,

E   She

She there shall drefs a fweeter fod
Than fancy's feet have ever trod.
By fairy hands their knell is rung,
By forms unfeen their dirge is fung,
There honour comes, a pilgrim grey,
To blefs the turf that wraps their clay;
And freedom fhall a while repair,
To dwell a weeping hermit there.

A 4 Voc. Dr. Cooke.

HARK! the lark at heav'n's gate fings,
    And Phœbus 'gins t'arife,
His fteeds to water at thofe fprings,
    On chalic'd flowers that lies.

And winking Marybuds begin
    To ope their golden eyes;
With ev'ry thing that pretty is,
    My lady fweet, arife.

A 4 Voc. Lord Mornington.

HERE in cool grot and moffy cell
    We rural fays and fairies dwell;
Tho' rarely feen by mortal eye,
When the pale moon afcending high,
Darts thro' yon limes her quiv'ring beams,
We frifk it near thefe cryftal ftreams;
Her beams reflected from the wave,
Afford the light our revels crave;

The turf with daisies 'broider'd o'er,
Exceeds, we wot, the Parian floor;
Nor yet for artful strains we call,
But listen to the water-fall.

A 4 Voc. Paxton.

HOW sweet, how fresh, this vernal day,
  How musical the air!
Nature was never seen so gay,
  Were but my Silvia near.
Hush! wanton birds, your am'rous song
  Alarms my virgin breast;
Retire, sweet whist'ling winds be gone,
  Retire, 'tis love's request.

A 4 Voc. Stafford Smith.

HARK! the hollow woods resounding,
  Echo to the hunter's cry;
Hark! how all the vales rebounding,
  To his cheering voice reply.
Now so swift o'er hills aspiring,
  He pursues the gay delight;
Distant woods and plains retiring,
  Seem to vanish from his sight.
Flying still, and still pursuing,
  See the fox, the hounds, the men,
Cunning cannot save from ruin;
  Far from refuge, wood, and den.

Now

Now they kill him—homeward hie them,
  For a jovial night's repaſt;
Thus no ſorrow e'er comes nigh them,
  Health continues to the laſt.

A 4 Voc. Webbe.

HAIL! happy meeting, vintage now is done,
    The grapes are purpled by the autumnal ſun;
Who having with his beams all nature bleſt,
Retires to Capricorn, and ſinks to reſt.
Now comes relentleſs Winter, that deforms
With froſt the foreſt, and the ſea with ſtorms;
We ſhun the rage, and thus in ſocial mirth,
We'll paſs our time till ſpring renews its birth:
Hail! happy meeting, crown'd with ev'ry bleſſing,
Thrice happy we ſuch plenty here poſſeſſing,
Each in his look his heart's content expreſſing.
Thus while together ſuch a treat before us,
Since it hath pleas'd great Bacchus to reſtore us,
Cantet nunc Io Amicorum chorus.

A 6 Voc. Webbe.

HENCE all ye vain delights!
   As ſhort as are the nights
  Wherein you ſpend your folly!
There's nought in this life ſweet,
If Man were wiſe to ſee't,
  But only Melancholy;
Oh! ſweeteſt Melancholy,

Welcome

Welcome folded arms and fixed eyes,
A figh that piercing, mortifies;
A look that's faften'd to the ground;
A tongue chain'd up—without a found:

Fountain heads, and pathlefs groves,
Places which pale paffion loves,
Moon-light walks, when all the fowls
Are fafely hous'd, fave bats and owls.

A midnight bell! a parting groan!
Thefe are the founds we feed upon!

Then ftretch our bones in a ftill, gloomy valley,
Nothing fo dainty fweet as Melancholy.

A 3 Voc.   FRANCIS IRELAND.

JOLLY Bacchus hear my pray'r,
     Vengeance on th' ungrateful fair;
In thy fmiling cordial bowl
Drown all the forrows of my foul;
Jolly Bacchus! fave! Oh fave!
From the deep devouring grave,
     A poor defpairing, fighing fwain.

Hafte, hafte away,
Lafh thy tygers, do not ftay,
I'm undone if thou delay.
If I view thofe eyes once more,
I ftill fhall love, and ftill adore,
And be more wretched than before.

A 4 Voc.   Dr. Cooke.

IN the merry month of May,
 In a morn by break of day,
Forth I walk'd by the wood fide,
Where, as May was in his pride,
There I fpied all alone
Phillida and Corydon :
Much ado there was, God wot,
For he would love, but fhe would not;
She faid, never man was true;
He faid, none was falfe to you;
He faid, he had lov'd her long;
She faid, love fhould have no wrong:
Corydon would kifs her then ;
She faid, maids muft kifs no men,
Till they did for good and all :
Then fhe made the fhepherd call
On all the heav'ns to witnefs truth,
That never lov'd a truer youth.
Thus with many a pretty oath,
Yea and nay, and faith and troth,
Such as filly fhepherds ufe,
When they will not love abufe :
Love, which had been long deluded,
Was with kiffes fweet concluded ;
And Phillida, with garland gay,
Was crown'd the Lady of the May.

A 4 Voc. Dr. Cooke.

IN paper cafe, hard by this place,
  Dead a poor dormoufe lies;
And foon or late, fummon'd by fate,
  Each prince, each monarch dies.

Ye fons of verfe, while we rehearfe,
  Attend inftructive rhime;
No fins had Dor to anfwer for,—
  Repent of your's in time.

A 3 Voc. Dr. Cooke.

I Have been young, though now grown old,
  Hardy in field, in battle bold.
I am young ftill, let who dares try,
I'll conquer or in combat die;
Whatever ye can do or tell,
I one day did you both excell.

A 6 Voc. Wilbye.

LADY, when I behold the rofes fprouting,
  Which clad in damafk mantles deck the arbours;
  And then behold your lips, where fweet love harbours,
Mine eyes prefent me with a double doubting;
For viewing both alike, hardly my mind fuppofes,
Whether the rofes be your lips, or your lips the rofes?

A 3

A 3 Voc. S. SMITH,

LET us, my Lesbia, live and love,
  Nor cast a moment's thought away;
Whether a peevish world approve,
  Or what they think, or what they say:

The sun that sets shall rise again;
  But when our short-liv'd day is o'er,
One long eternal night must reign,
  A lasting sleep — to wake no more!

Let us then live and love to-day,
And kiss the fleeting hours away.

A 4 Voc. WEBBE.

LIVE to-day, enjoy each blessing,
  Taking what the gods have sent;
Time is ever on us pressing,
  Let no moment be mispent:
Then fill the glass and fill the bowl,
  May Bacchus still with love agree;
And let each Briton warm his soul
  With Love, and Wine, and Liberty.

A 4 Voc. DR. HAYES.

MELTING airs soft joys inspire,
  Airs for drooping hope to hear;
Melting as a lover's pray'r,
Joys to flatter dull despair,
And softly soothe the am'rous fire.

A 4

A 4 Voc. Dr. Arne.

MAKE hafte to meet the gen'rous wine,
    Whofe piercing is for thee delay'd;
The rofy wreath is ready made, and artful hands prepare
The fragrant oil that fhall perfume thy hair.
Frefh rofes here with myrtles twine;
  But fimple all, without deceit,
    My wine from art is free,
  Which never woman was,
    Nor e'er will be.
When nectar fparkles from afar,
  And the free-hearted friend cries, come away,
Make hafte, refign thy bus'nefs and thy care,
  No mortal int'reft can be worth thy ftay.
Here Mirth refides, here Bacchus' rites are due,
Come, drink till ev'ry taper fhines like two;
Till whining love in bumpers deep be drown'd,
And all things, like the circling glafs, go round.

A 4 Voc. Rev. R. Greville.

NOW the bright morning ftar,
    Day's harbinger,
Comes dancing from the eaft,
And leads with her the flow'ry May;
Who from her green cap throws
The yellow cowflip and the pale primrofe.

A 4

A 4 Voc. WEBBE.

NOW I'm prepar'd to meet th' enchanting scene,
  This is the hour the happy guests convene;
Welcome this kind release from care,
What can to social joys compare?
With wine and songs the jovial night shall pass,
Till morning darts its rays into my glass;
When vine-crown'd Bacchus leads the way,
What can his votaries dismay?

A 5 Voc. MORLEY.

NOW is the month of maying,
  When merry lads are playing,
    Fa, la, la, la, la.
Each with his bonny lass,
A dancing on the grass;
    Fa, la, la, la, la.

A 4 Voc. T. NORRIS, M. B.

O'ER William's tomb, with silent grief opprest,
  Britannia mourns her hero now at rest;
Not tears alone, but praises too she gives,
Due to the guardian of our laws and lives:
Nor shall that laurel ever fade with years,
Whose leaves are water'd with a nation's tears.

A 3 Voc.   RAVENSCROFT.

OF all the brave birds that ever I fee,
  The owl is the faireft in her degree;
For all the day long fhe fits in a tree,
And when the night comes, away flies fhe:
      Te whit, te whoo,
      To whom drink'ft thou?
      Sir Noodle, to you!
This fong is well fung I make you a vow,
And he is a knave that drinketh now.
      Nofe, nofe;
And who gave thee that jolly red nofe?
      Cinnamon and ginger,
      Nutmeg and cloves,
And they gave me my jolly red nofe.

A 3 Voc.   WEBBE.

OFTEN in Laura's breaft I ftrove
  To plunge a dart quite full of love;
The dart, fo ftubborn is the fair,
Repell'd as oft, was loft in air;
Tell me, fweet mother, tell me why
Laura can thus my pow'r defy?
To Venus thus young Cupid cry'd,
To him the goddefs thus reply'd:
Have you not feen a caftle, boy,
  Elaftic hung with wool-packs round,
The cannon's wonted rage defy,
  And make the threat'ning ball rebound?

Thus,

Thus, when you shoot at Laura's heart,
The springing b—by turns the dart.

A Voc. Atterbury.

O Thou, sweet bird! that sits on some lone spray
   Unseen, amid yon solitary grove,
Fly to my love, and sing thy little lay,
   For lays like thine the hardest heart can move:
Sing, till around her soft-ey'd Pity play,
And one responsive sigh breathe sympathising love.

A 4 Voc. Callcott, M. B.

O Thou! where'er (thie bones att rest)
   Thie spryte to haunte delyghteth best,
Whether on the blod-embrued playne,
   Or where thou kenn'st from far
   The dysmal crye of war,
Or seest some mountayne made of hepes of slayne;
Or fierie rounde the mynsterne glare;
Let Bristowe stille bee made thie care:
Guarde itt fromme fomenne and consumynge fyre;
   Lyke Avon's streame encyrque itt rounde,
   Ne lette a flame enharme the grounde,
Tyll ynne one flame al the whole worlde expyre.

A 5

A 5 Voc. WEBBE.

PRETTY warbler, ceafe to hover,
  Pretty warbler, help a lover;
From thy joy a moment borrow,
Tune thy mufic to my forrow :
  Join and anfwer when I mourn.
To grieve alone is moft tormenting,
There's a pleafure in lamenting,
  My complaint if you return.

A 3 Voc. BAILDON.

PRITHEE, friend, fill t'other pipe,
  Fie for fhame don't let us part;
Juft when wit is brifk and ripe,
  Rais'd by wine's all-powerful art.
None but fools would thus retire
  To their drowfy fleepy bed;
Drawer, heap with coals the fire,
  Bring us t'other flafk of red.
Foot to foot then let us drink,
  Till things double to our view,
Pleafure then 'twill be to think,
  One full bumper looks like two :
Fill, my friend, then fill your glafs,
  Why fhould we at cares repine ?
Mifery crowns the fober afs,
  Happinefs the man of wine !

A 4 Voc. STAFFORD SMITH.

RETURN, bleſt days, return ye laughing hours,
 Which led me up the roſeate ſteep of youth,
Which ſtrew'd my ſimple path with vernal flow'rs,
 And bid me court chaſte ſcience and fair truth.
Witneſs ye winged daughters of the year,
 If e'er a ſigh had learnt to heave my breaſt,
If e'er my cheek was conſcious of a tear,
 Till Cynthia came, and robb'd my ſoul of reſt.
So ſoft, ſo delicate, ſo ſweet ſhe came,
 Youth's damaſk glow juſt dawning on her cheek;
I gaz'd, I ſigh'd, I caught the tender flame,
 Felt the fond pang, and droop'd with paſſion weak.

A 4 Voc. WEBBE.

RISE, my joy, ſweet mirth attend,
 I'm reſolv'd to be thy friend;
Sneaking Phoebus hides his head,
He's with Thetis gone to bed:
Tho' he will not on me ſhine,
Still there's brightneſs in the wine;
From Bacchus I'll ſuch luſtre borrow,
My face ſhall be a ſun to-morrow.

A 4 Voc. PAXTON.

ROUND the hapleſs Andrè's urn,
 Be the cypreſs foliage ſpread;
Fragrant ſpice profuſely burn,
 Honours grateful to the dead:

Let

Let a foldier's manly form,
   Guard the vafe his afhes bears ;
Truth in living forrow warm,
   Pay a mourning nation's tears :
Fame, his praife upon thy wing,
   Through the world difperfing tell ;
In the fervice of his King,
   In his Country's caufe he fell !

A 4 Voc. Dr. Hutchinson.

RETURN, return my lovely maid,
   For Summer's pleafures pafs away,
The trees green liv'ries 'gin to fade,
   And Flora's treafures all decay.
No more, at ev'n-tide, waileth fweet,
   Sad Philomel the woods among ;
Nor lark the rifing morn doth greet,
   Return, my love, thou ftay'ft too long.

A 5 Voc. Webbe.

SISTER of Phoebus, gentle queen,
   Of afpect mild, and ray ferene,
Whofe friendly beams by night appear,
The lonely traveller to cheer !
Attractive Power ! whofe mighty fway
The ocean's fwelling waves obey,
And, mounting upward, feem to raife
A liquid altar to thy praife :

                                  Thee,

Thee, wither'd hags, at midnight hour,
Invoke to their infernal bow'r:
But I to no such horrid rite,
Sweet queen, implore thy sacred light;
Nor seek, while all but lovers sleep,
To rob the miser's treasur'd heap:
Thy kindly beams alone impart,
To find the youth who stole my heart,
And guide me from thy silver throne,
To steal his heart — or find my own.

A 4 Voc.   Dr. Arne.

SWEET Muse! inspire thy suppliant bard,
  Heroic ardor to record.
In vain the fervent pray'r I move,
Hark! ev'ry echo whispers Love!
I'll raise the theme to acts renown'd ——
Ah! no, — 'tis Love, — no other found!
Farewell then, Patriot — Hero — King!
My Muse of nought but Love can sing.

A 5 Voc.   Stevens.

SIGH no more, ladies, sigh no more,
  Men were deceivers ever;
One foot on sea and one on shore,
  To one thing constant never.
Then sigh not so, but let them go,
  And be you blithe and bonny;
Converting all your sounds of woe,
  To hey nonny nonny.

Sing

Sing no more ditties, ladies, fing no more
  Of dumps fo dull and heavy,
The frauds of men were ever fo,
  Since fummer firft was leafy.
Then figh not, &c. &c.

A 4 Voc.   WEBBE.

SWIFTLY from the mountain's brow,
  Shadows nurs'd by night retire,
And the peeping fun-beams now
  Paint with gold the village fpire.

Sweet, O fwect, the warbling throng
  On the white embloffom'd fpray,
Nature's univerfal fong
  Echoes to the rifing day.

A 5 Voc.   ORLANDO GIBBONS.

THE filver fwan who living had no note,
  When death approach'd unlock'd her filent throat:
Leaning her breaft againft the reedy fhore,
Thus fung her firft and laft, and fung no more.
Farewell all joys, O death, come clofe mine eyes,
More geefe than fwans now live, more fools than wife.

A 3 Voc. WEELKES.

THE nightingale, the organ of delight,
 The nimble lark, the blackbird, and the thrush,
And all the pretty chorifters of flight,
 That chaunt their mufic notes on ev'ry bufh :
Let them no more contend who fhall excel ;
The cuckow is the bird that bears the bell.

A 3 Voc. WEBBE.

TO me the wanton girls infulting fay,
 Here in this glafs thy fading bloom furvey :
Juft on the verge of life, 'tis equal quite,
Whether my locks are black, or filver white ;
Rofes around my fragrant brows I'll twine,
And diffipate anxieties in wine.

A 4 Voc. WEBBE.

THE mighty conqueror of hearts,
 His pow'r I here deny ;
With all his flames, bis fires and darts,
 I, champion-like, defy.

I'll offer all my facrifice,
 Henceforth, at Bacchus' fhrine ;
The merry god ne'er tells us lies,
 There's no deceit in wine.

A 4

A 4 Voc. Webbe.

THE girl that I love is as mild as Aurora,
  Difcreet as Minerva, and youthful as Flora;
Rejoic'd at her prefence fond nature looks gay,
The trees bow their heads on each fide of her way.
The flow'rs fend forth a profufion of fweet,
The grafs looks more green, that is trod by her feet;
The birds hover round, as fhe trips it along,
And improve from her voice, the beft notes of her fong.
Great Phœbus himfelf is delighted to fee,
A pow'r more bright and more cheering than he;
And ftopping his fteeds in the midft of their way,
He gazes!— forgetting to drive on the day.

A 4 Voc. Danby,

THY breath as fragrant as her own confeft,
  Go, lovely rofe, and breathe in Delia's ear;
Expiring on her yet as lovely breaft,
  That beauty's bloffoms are as frail as fair.

A 3 Voc. Danby.

THE faireft flow'rs the vale prefer,
  And fhed ambrofial fweetnefs there;
While the tall pine and mountain oak,
Oft feel the tempeft's ruder ftroke:

So

So in the lowly mofs-grown feat,
  Dear peace and quiet dwell;
The ftorms that rack the rich and great,
  Fly o'er the fhepherd's cell.

A 3 Voc. BATTISHILL.

UNDERNEATH this myrtle fhade,
  On flow'ry beds fupinely laid,
With od'rous oils my head o'erflowing,
And around it rofes growing,
What fhould I do but drink away
The heat and troubles of the day?
In this more than kingly ftate,
Love himfelf fhall on me wait.
Fill to me, love, nay fill it up;
And mingled, caft into the cup
Wit, and mirth, and noble fires,
Vig'rous health, and gay defires.
Crown me with rofes whilft I live,
Now your wines and ointments give;
After death I nothing crave,
Let me alive my pleafures have,
All are ftoicks in the grave.

A 3 Voc. BAILDON.

WHEN gay Bacchus fills my breaft,
  All my cares are lull'd to reft;
Rich I feem as Lydia's king,
Merry catch, or ballad fing:

Ivy wreaths my temples shade,
Ivy, that will never fade;
Thus I sit in mind elate,
Laughing at the farce of state;
Some delight in fighting fields,
Nobler transports Bacchus yields;
Fill the bowl, I ever said,
'Tis better to lie drunk than dead.

A 5 Voc. Gir. Converso.

WHEN all alone my pretty love was playing,
    And I saw at a gaze, bright Phœbus staying,
Alas! I fear'd there would be some betraying.

A 4 Voc. S. Smith.

WHILE fools their time in stormy strife employ,
    Be ours engag'd in Union, Peace and Joy;
Thus the blest gods, the genial day prolong;
In feasts ambrosial, and celestial song;
Apollo tunes the lyre, the muses round,
With voice alternate, aid the silver sound.
Wisely we imitate the Pow'rs divine,
Peace at our heart, and pleasure our design.

A 5 Voc. WEBBE.

WHEN nature form'd that angel face,
　　She lavifh'd all her pow'r;
Be this, fhe cry'd, my mafter piece,
　　Kneel, mortals, and adore!

A 3 Voc. DANBY.

WHEN Sappho tun'd the raptur'd ftrain,
　　The lift'ning wretch forgot his pain;
With art divine, the lyre fhe ftrung,
Like thee fhe play'd, like thee fhe fung.
For when fhe ftruck the quiv'ring wire,
The eager breaft was all on fire;
But when fhe tun'd the vocal lay,
The captive foul was charm'd away.

A 3 Voc. CALLCOTT, M. B.

WHEN Arthur firft in court began
　　To wear long hanging fleeves,
He entertain'd three ferving men,
　　And all of them were thieves.

The firft he was an Irifhman,
　　The fecond was a Scot,
The third he was a Welchman,
　　And all were knaves I wot.

The

The Irishman lov'd Usquebaugh,
   The Scot lov'd Ale, call'd Blue Cap;
The Welchman, he lov'd Toasted Cheese,
   And made his mouth like a Mouse Trap.

Usquebaugh burnt the Irishman,
   The Scot was drown'd in ale;
The Welchman had like to be choak'd with a Mouse,
   But he pull'd her out by the tail.

A 5 Voc.   WEELKES.

WELCOME, sweet pleasure,
   My wealth and treasure;
To haste our playing,
There's no delaying,
   No no no no no!
This mirth delights me,
When sorrow spights me,
Then sing we all, Fa la la ;

Sorrow content thee,
Mirth must prevent thee ;
Though much thou grievest,
Thou none relievest,
   No no no no no!
Joy come delight me,
Though sorrow spight me,
Then sing we all, Fa la la.

Grief

Grief is difdainful,
Sottifh and painful;
Then wait on pleafure,
And lofe no leifure,
  No no no no no!
Heart's eafe it lendeth,
And comfort fendeth,
Then fing we all, Fa la la.

A 4 VOC.   EARL OF MORNINGTON.

WHEN for the world's repofe my faireft fleeps,
  See Cupid hovers round her couch and weeps;
Well may'it thou weep, proud boy, thy pow'r dies,
  Thou haft no dart when Chloe has no eyes.

A 4 VOC.   MORLEY.

WHITHER away fo faft my dear,
  From your true love approved;
What hafte, what hafte, I fay,
  Tell me my beft beloved?
Lo! then I come, difpatch thee
Hence away, or elfe I catch thee:
Think not thus to 'fcape without me,
But run and never doubt me.

A 3

A 3 Voc. *Publiſhed by* RAVENSCROFT.

WE be ſoldiers three,
   Pardonez moi je vous en prie;
Lately come forth from the low country,
   With never a penny of money.

Here, good fellow, I drink to thee,
   Pardonez moi je vous en prie;
To all good fellows, wherever they be,
   With never a penny of money.

And he that will not pledge me this,
   Pardonez moi je vous en prie;
Pays for the ſhot, what ever it is,
   With never a penny of money.

Charge it again, boy, charge it again,
   Pardonez moi je vous en prie;
As long as there is any ink in my pen,
   With never a penny of money.

A 3 Voc. Dr. ARNE.

WHEN Britain on her ſea-girt ſhore,
   Her ancient Druids firſt addreſt;
What aid, ſhe cry'd, ſhall I implore?
   What beſt defence, by numbers preſt?
Tho' hoſtile nations round thee riſe,
   (The myſtic Oracles reply'd)
And view thine Iſle with envious eyes,
   Their threats defy, their rage deride;

H

Nor fear invasion from those adverse Gauls,
Britain's best bulwarks are — her wooden walls.

Thine oaks descending to the main,
   With floating force shall stem the tides,
Asserting Britain's liquid reign,
   Where'er thy thund'ring navy rides.
Nor less to peaceful arts inclin'd,
   Where commerce opens all her stores,
In social bands shall lead mankind,
   And join the sea-divided shores ;
Spread then thy sails where naval glory calls,
Britain's best bulwarks are — her wooden walls.

Hail ! happy Isle, what tho' thy vales
   No vine-empurpled tribute yield,
Nor fann'd with odour-breathing gales,
   Nor crops spontaneous glad the field;
Yet Liberty rewards the toil
   Of Industry, to labour prone,
Who jocund ploughs the grateful soil,
   And reaps the harvest she has sown :
While other realms tyrannic sway enthralls,
Britain's best bulwarks are — her wooden walls.

A 4 Voc. WEBBE.

WHERE, hapless Ilion, are thy heav'n-built walls,
   Thy high embattled tow'rs, thy spacious halls ?
Where are thy temples, fill'd with forms divine ?
Where is thy Pallas ? where her awful shrine ?

The

The mighty Hector where? thy fav'rite boaft;
And all thy valiant fons, a fplendid hoft?
Thy arts, thy arms, thy riches, and thy ftate,
Thy pride, thy pomp, thy all that made thee great?
Thefe proftrate now in duft and ruin lie,
But thy tranfcendant fame can never die;
Fate boafts no pow'r to fink thy glories paft,
They fill the world, and with the world fhall laft.

A 4 Voc. S. Smith.

WHAT fhall we have that kill'd the deer?
　　His leathern fkin and horns to wear;
The horn, the horn, the lufty horn,
Is not a thing to laugh to fcorn.

Take you no fcorn to wear the horn,
It was a creft ere thou wert born;
Thy father's father wore it,
And thy father bore it:

The horn, the horn, the lufty horn,
Is not a thing to laugh to fcorn.

A 4 Voc. Morley.

WITHIN an arbour of fweet-briar and rofes,
　　I heard two lovers talking wanton cofes;
Say, lovely maid, quoth he, to whom is thy liking ty'd?
To whom but thee, my deareft life, the gentle nymph
　　　　reply'd!

H 2　　　　　　　　　　　I die,

I die, I die, I die, quoth he;
And I, and I, and I, faid fhe;
Ah! give me, give me then, quoth he, fome token,
And with his hands the reft he would have fpoken:
Fie! away then, cry'd the nymph; alas! too well you
know it;
Ah! quoth he, fweetly come kifs me, then; kifs me,
and — fhow it.

A 5 Voc.   WEBBE.

YOU gave me your heart t'other day,
I thought it as fafe as my own;
I've not loft it, — but, what can I fay?
Not your heart from mine can be known!

A 3 Voc.   *Publifhed by* RAVENSCROFT.

WE be three poor mariners,
Newly come from the feas,
We fpend our lives in jeopardy,
While others live at eafe:
Shall we go dance the round, around, around,
And he that is a bully, boy,
Come pledge me on this ground.
We care not for thofe martial men,
That do our ftates difdain,
But we care for thofe merchantmen,
Which do our ftates maintain;

To

To them we dance this round, around, around,
   And he that is a bully, boy,
   Come pledge me on this ground.

A 3 Voc. L. MARENZIO.

WILL you hear how once repining,
   Great Eliza captive lay,
Each ambitious thought refigning,
   Foe to riches, pomp, and fway.
While the nymphs and fwains delighted,
   Tript around in all their pride;
Envying joys, by others flighted,
   Thus the Royal Maiden cry'd.

Hark! to yonder milk-maid, finging
   Cheerly o'er the brimming pail;
Cowflips all around her fpringing,
   Sweetly paint the golden vale.
Never yet did courtly maiden,
   Move fo fprightly, look fo fair;
Never breaft with jewels laden,
   Pour a fong fo void of care.

Would indulgent heav'n had granted
   Me fome rural damfel's part;
All the empire I had wanted,
   Then had been my fhepherd's heart.
Then, with him, o'er hills and mountains,
   Free from fetters might I rove,
Fearlefs tafte the chryftal fountains,
   Peaceful fleep beneath the grove.

A 5

A 5 Voc. Webbe.

WHEN winds breathe foft along the filent deep,
　The waters curl, the peaceful billows fleep:
A ftronger gale the troubled wave awakes;
The furface roughens, and the ocean fhakes.
More dreadful ftill, when furious ftorms arife,
The mounting billows bellow to the fkies;
On liquid rocks the tott'ring veffel's tofs'd,
Unnumber'd furges lafh the foaming coaft:
The raging waves, excited by the blaft,
Whiten with wrath, and fplit the fturdy maft,
When in an inftant, he who rules the floods,
Earth, air, and fire, Jehovah, God of gods,
In pleafing accents fpeaks his fovereign will,
And bids the waters, and the winds, be ftill!
Hufh'd are the winds, the waters ceafe to roar;
Safe are the feas, and filent as the fhore.
Now fay what joy elates the failor's breaft,
With profp'rous gales fo unexpected bleft:
What eafe, what tranfport, in each face is feen,
The heav'ns look bright, the air and fea ferene:
For ev'ry plaint we hear a joyful ftrain
To Him, whofe pow'r unbounded rules the main.

A 3 Voc. Baildon.

WHAT Anacreon lov'd we drink,
　Prefs it clofely to the lip;
Mifers, can ye fleep or think,
　While fuch nectar here we fip?

Our gay honeſt Horace would take off his flaſk,
  While Ovid in love play'd the fool:
Come, broach the Falernian or Maſſic old caſk,
  And follow gay Horace's rule.

Let the whining lover ſigh,
  All his tears are ſhed in vain;
But a bumper can ſupply,
  Ev'ry tear that love can drain.

Love was ne'er a treaſure,
Drinking is a pleaſure,
  Then fill your gen'rous goblet high!
Let your glaſſes gingle
Thus our joys we mingle,
  Drink, ſons of Bacchus, till ye die.

A 3 VOC. DR. ARNE.

YOU aſk me, dear Jack, for an emblem that's rife,
  And clearly explains the true medium of life:
I think I have hit it, as ſure as a gun,
A bowl of good Punch and the Medium are one.
When Lemon and Sugar ſo happily meet,
The acid's corrected by mixing the ſweet;
The water and ſpirit ſo luckily blend,
That each from th' extreme doth the other defend.
Then fill up the bowl, rot ſorrow and ſtrife,
A bumper! my boys, to the Medium of Life:
Which keeps our frail ſtate in a temper that's meet,
Contented in blending the ſour with the ſweet.

A 3

A 3 Voc. Webbe.

O Come O bella l'ardor de vini,
    Piu coralini tuoi la bri fa,
Bacco vi ſtilla, ſuave umore,
    D'un tal ſapore che amor non ha,
Bevil' O cara, quando ha la ſpuma,
    Tal ſi coſtuma guſtarlo qui,
Coſi gridando l'ama il franceſe,
    Cheto l'Ingleſe l'ama coſi.
Ma cara luci voi non vedete,
    Qual altra ſiete ſui l'abri ſta,
Aita il core ch' è tutto fuoco,
    Et a poco a poco mancando va.
Si bella Dori godiam che il giorno,
    Preſto è al ritorno preſto al partir,
Di giovanezza godiam il fiore,
    Poi l'ultim' ore laſciam venir.

A 4 Voc. Callcott, M. B.

THYRSIS when he left me ſwore,
    In the ſpring he would return ;
Ah! what means that op'ning flow'r,
    And the bud that decks the thorn ?
'Twas the nightingale that ſung,
'Twas the lark that upward ſprung.

Idle notes, untimely green,
    Why ſuch unavailing haſte ?
Gentle gales and ſky ſerene,
    Prove not always winter paſt ;

Ceaſe

Ceafe my doubts, my fears remove;
Spare the honour of my love.

An 8 Voc. DANBY.

ODE TO HOPE.

THOU bleffing fent us from above,
  Rich offspring of celeftial love,
Fair Hope! thy prefence let me hail,
When grief intrudes, when pains affail:
On life's rough fea, amid the tempeft's roar,
Pilot my rolling bark, and fet me fafe on fhore.

A 3 Voc. CALLCOTT, M. B.

PEACE to the fouls of the heroes,
  Their deeds were great in fight;
Let them ride around me on clouds,
Let them fhew their features in war;
My foul then fhall be firm in danger,
And mine arm like the thunder of heav'n:
But be thou on a moon-beam, O Morna,
Near the window of my reft,
When my thoughts are of peace,
When the din of arms is paft.

I

A 4

A 4 Voc. Callcott, M. B.

TRIUMPHANT love, with roseate garlands crown'd,
  Has tun'd my lyre to hope's delightful theme ;
Applauding virtue casts a lustre round,
  And tells the world such bliss is bliss supreme.

A 4 Voc. Stevens.

YE spotted snakes with double tongue,
  Thorny hedge-hogs, be not seen ;
Newts and blind worms, do no wrong,
  Come not near our fairy queen :
    Philomel with melody,
    Sing in your sweet lullaby.

Weaving spiders come not near,
  Hence ! ye long-leg'd spinners, hence !
Beetles black, approach not near,
  Worm and snail do no offence :
    Philomel with melody,
    Sing in your sweet lullaby.

A 4 Voc. Danby,

THE nightingale who tunes her warbling notes so sweet,
  'Midst flow'rs ne'er presumes to fix her mournful seat ;
Melodiously she sings, while hawthorns pierce her breast,
Her voice sweet echo rings, and nature lulls to rest.

A 5

A 5 Voc. CALLCOTT, M. B.

O Voi che fofpirate a miglior notti
   Ch' afcoltate d'amore,
 O dite in rime,
Pregate non mi fia piu forda morte,
   Parto delle miferie
   E fin del pianto.

A 5 Voc. STEVENS.

IT was a lover and his lafs,
   With a hey, and a ho, and a hey nonino,
That o'er the green corn-fields did pafs
   In the fpring time;
The pretty fpring time, when birds do fing,
Hey ding a ding, fweet lovers love the fpring.

And therefore take the prefent time,
   With a hey, and a ho, and a hey nonino,
For love is crown'd with the prime,
   In the fpring time;
The pretty fpring time, when birds do fing,
Sweet lovers love the fpring.

A 3 Voc. WEBBE.

NON fide al mar che freme,
   La temeraria prora,
Chi fi fcolora e teme,
   Sol quando vede il mar:

Non

Non fi cimenti in Campo,
Chi trema al fuono e al lampo;
D'una guerriera tromba
D'un bellicoro acciar.

A 4 Voc. Callcott, M. B.

ARE the white hours for ever fled,
  That us'd to mark the cheerful day?
And ev'ry blooming pleafure dead,
  That led th' enraptur'd foul aftray?
Too faft the rofy-footed train,
  The bleft delicious moments paft:
Pleafure muft now give way to pain,
  And grief fucceed to joy at laft.
O! daughters of eternal Jove,
  Return with the returning year;
Bring pleafure back, and fmiles, and love,
  Let blooming love again appear.

A 3 Voc. Sacchini,

HOW fhould we mortals fpend our hours?
  In War, in Love, and Drinking!
None but a fool confumes his pow'rs
  In Peace, in Care, and Thinking.

Time, would you let him wifely pafs,
  Is lively, brifk, and jolly:
Dip but his wing in the fparkling glafs,
  And he'll drown dull Melancholy.

A 5

A 5 Voc. DANBY.

ROSY finger'd goddefs rife,
  Fair Aurora, mount the fkies;
Leave, O leave, your chryftal bed,
Deck'd with coral beauteous red;
From each bufh the feather'd choir,
Warbling fweet, new joys infpire;
Warbling fweet, each myrtle grove
Returns to meet the god of love:
Come then, fhepherds, come away!
Come, ye damfels fair and gay;
Releafe your herds and fnowy fheep,
That they the pearly dew may fip:
More grateful to the thirfty flocks
Than to Narcifs' his golden locks.
Come, ere Sol's effervent beams
Parch the fields, or heat the ftreams;
Clad each in his beft array,
We'll celebrate this holiday;
Dancing, mufic, cheerful fong,
Shall the fleeting hours prolong.

A 4 Voc. DANBY.

SWEET thrufh, that makes the vernal year
  Sweeter than Flora can appear;
As Philomel attends thy lay,
She envies the return of day.

The

The tuneful lyre and fwelling flute,
At thy rich warbling fhall be mute;
Vocal minftrell, thy foft lay
Treafures up, and ends the May:
Hark! how the blackbird woo's his love,
The fkill'd mufician of the grove;
On thorn, as perch'd, he nobly fings,
A cadence for the beft of kings;
Sublime and foft, gay and ferene,
A virginal to hail a queen:
Nature's mufic thus improves,
All the graces and the loves.

A 4 Voc.   Webbe.

CUPID, my pleafure, foft love I thee implore;
   Bacchus, my treafure, brifk wine I will adore:
Give me a beautiful maid to blefs my longing arms!
Give me a bumper of red, in that I view all charms.
Without thy joy, life foon would cloy,
   And prove a mere difeafe;
The noble juice will mirth produce,
   And give us eafe.

A 3 Voc.   Callcott, M. B.

I.

FROM thy waves, ftormy Lannow, I fly,
   From the rocks that are lafh'd by their tide;
From the nymph whofe cold bofom, relentlefs as they,
   Has wreck'd my warm hopes by her pride;

Yet

Yet lonely, and rude as the fcene,
  Her fmile to that fcene cou'd impart
A charm that might rival the bloom of the vale;
  But, away thou fond dream of my heart!
        To thy rocks, ftormy Lannow, adieu.

II.

Now the blafts of the winter come on,
  And the waters grow dark as the fkies;
But, 'tis well! they refemble the fullen difdain
  That has lour'd in thofe infolent eyes:
Sincere were the fighs it reprefs'd,
  But they rofe in the days that are flown,
Ah! nymph unrelenting, and cold as thou art,
  My fpirit is proud as thine own.
        To thy rocks, ftormy Lannow, adieu.

III.

Now the wings of the fea-fowl are fpread,
  To efcape the rough ftorm by their flight;
And thefe caves will afford them a gloomy retreat
  From the wind, and the billows of night.
Like them, to the home of my youth,
  Like them, to the fhades I'll retire;
Receive me! and fhield my vex'd fpirit, ye groves,
  From the pangs of infulted defire.
        To thy rocks, ftormy Lannow, adieu.

A 6 Voc. Webbe.

Ode on St. Cecilia.

CECILIA more than all the mufes fkill'd,
 Phœbus himfelf muft to her yield ;
And at her feet lay down
His golden harp and laurel crown :
The foft enervate lyre is drown'd
In the deep organ's more majeftic found ;
In peals the fwelling notes afcend the fkies,
Perpetual breath the fwelling notes fupplies :
 And lafting as her name,
 Who form'd the tuneful frame,
Th' immortal mufic never dies !

A 4 Voc. Corfe.

I.

WHAT beauties does Flora difclofe!
 How fweet are her fmiles upon Tweed !
Yet Mary's ftill fweeter than thofe,
 Both nature and fancy exceed.
No daify nor fweet blufhing rofe,
 Nor all the gay flow'rs of the field ;
Not Tweed gliding gently thro' thofe,
 Such beauty and pleafure does yield.

II.

II.

'Tis she does the virgins excel,
  No beauty with her may compare;
Love's graces all round her do dwell,
  She's faireft where thoufands are fair.
Say, Charmer, where do thy flocks ftray?
  Oh! tell me at noon where they feed?
Shall I feek them on fweet winding Tay,
  Or the pleafanter banks of the Tweed?

A 3 Voc.   Corfe.

IN the hall I lay in night,
  Mine eyes half clos'd with fleep;
Soft mufic came to mine ear;
It was the maid of Selma.
Her neck was white as the bofom of a fwan
Trembling on fwift rolling waves:
She rais'd the nightly fong;
For fhe knew that my foul was a ftream
That flow'd at pleafant founds.
Mix'd with the harp, arofe her voice;
She came on my troubled foul
Like a beam on the dark heaving ocean,
When it burfts from a cloud,
And brightens the foamy fide of a wave;
'Twas like the mem'ry of joys that are paft,
Pleafant and mournful to the foul!

K   A 4

A 4 Voc. Corfe.

I.

BENEATH a green fhade a lovely young fwain,
  One ev'ning reclin'd to difcover his pain;
So fad, yet fo fweetly he warbled his woe,
The wind ceas'd to breathe, and the fountains to flow:
Rude winds, with compaffion, could hear him complain,
Yet Chloe, lefs gentle, was deaf to his ftrain!

II.

How happy, he cry'd, my moments once flew,
Ere Chloe's bright charms firft flafh'd in my view;
Thefe eyes then with pleafure the dawn could furvey,
Nor fmil'd the fair morning more cheerful than they:
Now fcenes of diftrefs pleafe only my fight,
I'm tortur'd in pleafure, and languifh in light.

A 5 Voc. Stevens.

O! miftrefs mine, where are you roaming?
  O! ftay and hear, your true love's coming,
 That can fing both high and low:
Trip no further, pretty fweeting,
Journeys end in lovers meeting,
  Ev'ry wife man's fon doth know.

What is love? 'tis not hereafter;
Prefent mirth has prefent laughter,

What's

What's to come is still unsure:
In delay there lies no plenty,
Then don't leave me, sweet and twenty,
　　Youth's a season won't endure.

———————————

A 4 Voc.　Corfe.

IN April, when primroses paint the sweet plain,
　And summer approaching rejoiceth the swain,
The yellow-hair'd laddie would often-times go,
To wilds and deep glens, where the hawthorn trees grow:

There, under the shade of an old sacred thorn,
With freedom he sung his love ev'ning and morn;
He sung with so soft and enchanting a sound,
That silvans and fairies unseen danc'd around.

———————————

A 3 Voc.　Callcott, M. B.

AS I was going to Derby,
　　'Twas on a market-day,
I met the finest ram, Sir,
　　That ever was fed upon hay;
This ram was fat behind, Sir,
　　This ram was fat before,
This ram was ten yards high, Sir,
　　Indeed, he was no more!

The

The butcher that kill'd this ram, Sir,
 Was up to his knees in blood!
The boy that held the pail, Sir,
 Was carried away by the flood!
The tail that grew upon his rump
 Was ten yards and an ell,
And that was fent to Derby,
 To toll the market bell.

A 3 Voc.   BAILDON.

MR. Speaker! though 'tis late,
 I muft lengthen the debate.
Queftion — Order — hear him, hear!
Pray fupport, fupport the chair!
Sir, I fhall name you if you ftir.

A 4 Voc.   R. COOKE.

NO riches from his fcanty ftore
 My lover could impart;
He gave me a boon I valu'd more,
 He gave me all his heart.
But now for me, in fearch of gain,
 From fhore to fhore he flies;
Why wander riches to obtain,
 When love is all I prize!

A 4 Voc. HINDLE.

QUEEN of the filver bow! by thy pale beam,
  Alone and penfive, I delight to ftray;
And watch thy fhadow trembling in the ftream,
  Or mark the floating clouds that crofs thy way.
Still while I gaze, thy mild and placid light
  Sheds a foft calm upon my troubled breaft;
And oft I think, fair planet of the night,
  That in thy orb the wretched may have reft.
The fuff'rers of the earth, perhaps, may go,
  Releas'd by death, to thy benignant fphere;
And the fad children of defpair and woe,
  Forget in thee their cup of forrow here.
O! that I foon may reach thy world ferene,
Poor wearied pilgrim in this toiling fcene.

A 3 Voc. WEBBE.

AWAY! away! we've crown'd the day,
  The hounds are waiting for their prey:
The huntfman's call invites ye all,
  Come in, boys, while ye may

The jolly horn, the rofy morn,
  With harmony of deep-mouth'd hounds:
For thefe, my boys, are fportfman's joys,
  Our pleafure knows no bounds.

A 5 Voc. Danby.

AS paffing by a fhady grove,
  I heard a linnet fing,
Whofe fweetly plaintive voice of love
  Proclaim'd the cheerful fpring.
His pretty accents feem'd to flow
  As if he knew no pain ;
His downy throat he tun'd fo fweet,
  It echo'd o'er the plain.
Ah ! happy warbler, I reply'd,
  Contented thus to be ;
'Tis only harmony and love
  Can be compar'd with thee.

A 5 Voc. Callcott, M. B.

FATHER of heroes ! high dweller of eddying winds,
  Where the dark-red thunder marks the troubled clouds ;
Open thou thy ftormy halls ;
Let the bards of old be near.
We fit at the rocks, but there is no voice ;
  No light but the meteor of fire.
O ! from the rock on the hill,
From the top of the windy fteep,
O ! fpeak, ye ghofts of the dead !
O ! whither are ye gone to reft ?
In what cave of the hill fhall we find the departed ?
  No feeble voice is on the gale ;
  No anfwer half-drown'd in the ftorm !

Father

Father of heroes! the people bend before thee;
Thou turneſt the battle in the field of the brave;
   Thy terrors pour the blaſts of death!
   Thy tempeſts are before thy face!
   But thy dwelling is calm, above the clouds;
   The fields of thy reſt are pleaſant.

A 3 Voc.   WEBBE.

TO the old, long life and treaſure;
   To the young, all health and pleaſure;
  To the fair, their face
  With eternal grace,
And the reſt to be lov'd at leiſure.

A 5 Voc.   CALLCOTT, M. B.

HAIL, happy Albion! queen of Iſles!
   Peaceful freedom o'er thee ſmiles:
Thy lib'ral heart, thy judging eye,
The flow'r unheeded can deſcry,
And bid it round heav'n's altars ſhed
The fragrance of its bluſhing head.

Through the wild waves as they roar,
With watchful eye and dauntleſs mien,
Thy ſteady courſe of honour keep;
Nor fear the rocks, nor ſeek the ſhore,
The ſtar of Brunſwick ſhines ſerene,
And gilds the horrors of the deep.

A 4

A 4 Voc.　J. C. Pring.

AS I wove with wanton care,
　　Fillets for a virgin's hair ;
Cupid, and I mark'd him well,
Hid him in a cowflip's bell.
While he plum'd a pointed dart,
Fated to inflame the heart ;
Glowing with malicious joy,
Sudden I fecur'd the boy :
And, regardlefs of his cries,
Bore the little frighted prize
Where the mighty goblet ftood,
Teeming with a rofy flood.
Urchin ! in my rage I cry'd,
What avails thy faucy pride ?
Thus, I drown thee in my cup —
Thus, in wine I drink thee up !

A 3 Voc.　Dr. Cooke.

STAY, lovely Laura, ftay, let us fit and play,
　　While Phœbus hurries on the fultry day.
Let us the whifp'ring pines' cool fhade enjoy ;
How foft they murmur as the Zephyrs figh !
While the brook, bubbling to my pipe's foft charms,
Shall woo fome gentle vifion to thy arms.

CHLOE found Amyntas lying,
 All in tears upon the plain ;
Sighing to himself and crying,
 Wretched I ! to love in vain.
Ever fcorning and denying
 To reward a faithful fwain ;
Kifs, me dear, before my dying,
Kifs me once, and eafe my pain.

Chloe, laughing at his crying,
 Told him that he lov'd in vain ;
But, repenting and complying,
 When he kifs'd, fhe kifs'd again :
Kifs'd him up before his dying,
Kifs'd him up, and eas'd his pain.

A 3 Voc.   WEBBE.

SEE ! with ivy chaplet bound,
 And wreaths of vernal rofes crown'd,
Bacchus comes, and brings along
Blooming mirth and cheerful fong :
But, ah ! no myrtle there is feen,
No laurel fpreads a lafting green !
Say, does Apollo fly the train ?
Or lovely Venus, wine difdain ?
Behold the mufes now appear,
And willing beauty fighs fincere ;
Happier far than gods above,
We fill to Harmony and Love ;

L

Happier far than men below,
Now with sparkling wine we glow:
Happier still our lot shall be,
Bleft with these and Liberty.

A 4 Voc. WEBBE.

SINCE harmony deigns with her vot'ries to dwell,
    Exalt ev'ry voice, and each note loudly swell;
Intreat her to visit us here ev'ry night,
And thus by her presence diffuse new delight;
And since she such mirth and such pleasure can bring,
Let us Io Pœan repeatedly sing.

A 3 Voc. JACKSON, *Exon.*

THOU, to whose eyes I bend; at whose command,
    Tho' low my voice, tho' artless be my hand:
I take the sprightly reed, and sing or play,
Careless of all the cens'ring world may say.
O, fairest of thy sex, be thou my muse,
Deign on my work thine influence to diffuse;
So shall my notes to future times proclaim,
Unbounded love and ever-during flame.

A 3 Voc. JACKSON, *Exon.*

ON a day, alack! the day,
    Love, whose month was ever May,
Spy'd a blossom passing fair,
Playing in the wanton air: Thro'

Thro' the velvet leaves the wind,
All unseen, 'gan passage find,
That the lover, sick to death,
Wish'd himself the heaven's breath.
Air, quoth he, thy cheeks may blow;
Air, would I might triumph so!
But, alas! my hand hath sworn
Ne'er to pluck thee from thy thorn;
Vow, alack! for youth unmeet,
Youth so apt to pluck a sweet;
Thou, for whom e'en Jove would swear,
Juno but an Ethiop were;
And deny himself for Jove,
Turning mortal for thy love.

A 3 Voc. JACKSON, *Exon.*

IN a vale clos'd with woodland, where grottoes abound,
  Where rivulets murmur, and echoes resound;
I vow'd to the muses my time and my care,
Since neither could win me the smiles of my fair.

As freedom inspir'd me, I rang'd and I sung,
And Daphne's dear name never fell from my tongue;
But if a smooth accent delighted my ear,
I could wish unawares that my Daphne might hear.

With fairest ideas my bosom I stor'd,
To drive from my heart the fair nymph I ador'd;
But the more I with study my fancy refin'd,
The deeper impression she made on my mind.

Ah!

Ah! whilft I the beauties of nature purfue,
I ftill muft my Daphne's fair image renew;
The graces have chofen with Daphne to rove,
And the mufes are all in alliance with love!

A 4 Voc.   Dr. Cooke.

LONG may live my lovely Hetty,
    Always young, and always pretty.

A 4 Voc.   Danby,

NOR blazing gems, nor filken fheen,
    Befpeak the wearer's heart ferene;
Nor purple robe, nor tiffued veft,
Proclaim the calm unruffled breaft.
The crimfon mantle, and the jewell'd crown,
Fair peace forfakes, well pleas'd to own
The fhepherd's fimple garb and ruffet gown.
Sweet peace forfakes the crouded ftreet,
And fhelters in the calm retreat;
With folitude the charmer dwells,
'Midft rural meads and flow'ry dells:
She fhuns the coftly feaft, and rare,
Contented with the fhepherd's fare;
She fcorns the roofs where nobles dwell,
And feeks the ruftic's humbler cell;
She flights the mifer's glitt'ring hoard,
The joys of wine, and plenteous board;
Fair virtues livery fhe wears,
And all the joys of life are hers.

A 3

A 3 Voc. WEBBE.

O ! what can equal here below,
  The life of us three brothers!
The rifing figh of burfting woe,
  The balm of friendfhip fmothers.
The ftream of life fo fmoothly flows,
  We fcarcely feel it gliding ;
No dang'rous wave the current knows,
  Our bark with harm betiding :
Nor anxious thought, nor teafing care,
  Our peace of mind deftroying ;
The focial glafs we freely fhare,
  Thus doubly life enjoying.
In friendfhip's ties fo firmly bound,
  Misfortune's ftorms we weather,
And ev'ry blaft that would confound,
  Unites us more together.

A 3 Voc. CALLCOTT, M. B.

WHILE the moon-beams, all bright,
  Give a luftre to night,
I'll weep on his dwelling fo narrow,
And high o'er his grave,
The willow trees wave,
  Who died on the banks of the Yarrow.

'Twas under this fhade,
Hand in hand as we ftray'd,

He

He fell by the flight of an arrow;
And faft from the wound,
His blood ftain'd the ground,
Who died on the banks of the Yarrow.

A 3 Voc. WEBBE.

M^{R.} ———— will you do us the favour
    To join in a catch? Sir, I'll do my endeavour:
To be fure I've a cold, — but I'll ftill do my beft;
As I know your intention, I'll join with the reft.
May the fmiles of the company thus ever cheer us,
And we all give pleafure to thofe who may hear us.

A 3 Voc. CALLCOTT, M. B.

THOU, who alone doft all my thoughts infufe,
    And art at once my miftrefs and my mufe;
Infpir'd from thee flows every facred line,
Thine is the poetry, the poetry thine;
Thy fervice fhall my only bus'nefs be,
And all my life employ'd in pleafing thee.

A 4 Voc. CALLCOTT, M. B.

LOVELY feems the moon's fair luftre
    To the loft benighted fwain,
When all filv'ry bright fhe rifes,
    Gilding mountain, grove, and plain.

Lovely

Lovely feems the fun's full glory
  To the fainting feaman's eyes,
When fome horrid ftorm difperfing,
  O'er the wave his radiance flies.

A 3 Voc. CALLCOTT, M. B.

I.

YOU, gentlemen of England, that live at home at eafe,
  Ah! little do you tnink upon the dangers of the feas;
Give ear unto the mariners, and they will plainly fhow,
All the cares and the fears, when the ftormy winds do blow.

II.

If enemies oppofe us, when England is at wars
With any foreign nations, we fear not wounds nor fcars,
Our roaring guns fhall teach 'em our valour for to know,
Whilft they reel on the keel, when the ftormy winds do blow.

III.

Then, courage all brave mariners, and never be difmay'd,
Whilft we have bold adventurers we ne'er fhall want a trade;
Our merchants will employ us to fetch them wealth we know,
Then be bold, work for gold, when the ftormy winds do blow.

A 4 Voc. WEBBE.

GREAT Apollo, ftrike the lyre,
  Fill the raptur'd foul with fire!
Let the feftive fong go round,
Let this night with joy be crown'd.

                                    Hark!

Hark ! what numbers foft and clear,
Steal upon the ravifh'd ear !
Sure, no mortal fweeps the ftrings ;
Liften ! — 'tis Apollo fings !

A 3 Voc.   WEBBE.

I'll enjoy the prefent time,
 I'll be merry while I may ;
Love away youth's gentle prime,
 Ever happy, ever gay.

Youth's the feafon made for love,
 Love's the fource of blifs below ;
I'll the pleafing fpan improve,
 Nor wafte one precious hour in woe.

Too foon old age, with gloomy care,
 This fweet tranfporting fcene deftroys ;
And filvers o'er my wanton hair,
 And robs me of thofe fleeting joys.

A 4 Voc.   WEBBE.

GODDESS of the cheerful fmile,
 Thou can'ft ev'ry care beguile !
Still to me thy joys impart,
Raife the fpirits, warm the heart ;
Fix thine empire in my breaft,
Still an ever welcome gueft.

A 3 Voc.   Callcott, M. B.

WHO comes, so dark, from ocean's roar,
    Like Autumn's shadowy cloud?
Death is trembling in his hand,
His eyes are flames of fire!

Son of the cloudy night, retire;
Call thy winds and fly;
Retire thou to thy cave.

But let us sit by the mossy fount,
Let us hear the mournful voice of the breeze,
When it sighs on the grass of the cave.

A 3 Voc.   Webbe.

SURLY Giles's old cat was shut out of the house;
    How she plagu'd him all night without catching a mouse!
With her mew, sick to death, surly Giles rose in haste,
And vow'd that no longer his moments he'd waste;
So he took up a stick as he jump'd out of bed,
And swore he would knock the old cat o' the head.

A 3 Voc.   Reginald Spofforth.

SEE, smiling from the rosy east,
    The harbinger of day
Pours with majestic lustre dress'd
    The treasures of his ray:

M

No more her charms Aurora ſhrouds
Behind the ſullen veil of clouds ;
But ſheds profuſe her animating pow'rs,
And from their wint'ry ſleep, awakes the flow'rs,

A 3 Voc. Webbe.

AWAKE, ſweet muſe! the breathing ſpring
With rapture warms, awake and ſing ;
Awake, and join the vocal throng,
Who hail the morning with a ſong.
To Nancy raiſe the cheerful lay,
O bid her haſte, and come away :
In ſweeteſt ſmiles herſelf adorn,
And add new graces to the morn.

A 3 Voc. Webbe.

WHAT may arrive of care to-morrow
Let dull and vulgar ſouls divine ;
And joyleſs brood o'er future ſorrow,
While here we drown the paſt in wine.
The bowl ſupplies eternal ſtreams of pleaſure
To him who wiſely filling, takes his meaſure.

A 4 Voc. Webbe, jun.

WHEN pearly dew, at early dawn,
 Hangs pendant from the blooming thorn,
The lark to usher in the morn
 Awakes the feather'd throng:
Borne upwards on her tender wings,
As from the sod she eager springs,
In softest numbers sweetly sings
 Her grateful morning song.

A 5 Voc. Webbe.

THE blossom so pleasing at summer's gay call,
 Must languish at first, and must afterwards fall:
But behind it the fruit its successor shall rise
By nature disrob'd of its beauteous disguise.
So, Celia, when youth, that gay blossom is o'er,
By her virtues improv'd shall engage me the more;
Shall recall ev'ry beauty that brighten'd her prime,
When her merit is ripen'd by love and by time.

A 4 Voc. Webbe, jun.

SWEET stream, that winds thro' yonder glade,
 Apt emblem of a virtuous maid;
Silent and pure she glides along,
Far from the world's gay busy throng:

With

With gentle yet prevailing force,
Intent upon her deſtin'd courſe ;
Graces attend on all ſhe does,
Bleſſing and bleſt where e'er ſhe goes.

F I N I S.

INDEX.

Come,

INDEX.

Go,

INDEX.

Lady,

INDEX.

N

INDEX.

INDEX.

www.ingramcontent.com/pod-product-compliance
Lightning Source LLC
Chambersburg PA
CBHW020035030726
47499CB00007B/2438